Ginger McFlea
will not clean her teeth

A Lothian Children's Book

Published in Australia and New Zealand in 2010
by Hachette Australia Pty Ltd
Level 17, 207 Kent Street, Sydney NSW 2000
www.hachettechildrens.com.au

National Library of Australia
Cataloguing-in-Publication data:

Fox, Lee.

Ginger McFlea will not clean her teeth / author, Lee Fox ;
illustrator, Mitch Vane.

978 0 7344 1105 1 (hbk.)
978 0 7344 1129 7 (pbk.)

For children.
Vane, Mitch.

A823.4

Designed by Raylee Sloane, Kinart
Original concept by Pigs Might Fly
Colour reproduction by Splitting Image
Printed in China by Toppan Leefung Printing Ltd

Ginger McFlea will not clean her teeth

Lee Fox and Mitch Vane

LOTHIAN
Children's Books

For my delightful daughter Caitlin
L.F.

For my darling Mum,
you are with me in everything I do
M.V.

Ginger McFlea
will **not** clean her teeth.

She gives
her toothbrush
to her
pet turtle
Keith,

and says to her mum,
'It got pinched
by a thief!'

But Ginger McFlea
will **not** clean her teeth.

Ginger McFlea
will **not** clean
her choppers.

While
Jasper's
example is
glowing
and
proper,

she eats
chewy toffees

and
sticky
gobstoppers.

Her cavities soon
become massive
big whoppers.

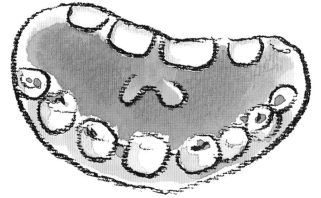

But Ginger McFlea
will **not** clean her choppers.

Ginger McFlea
will **not**
clean her pegs.

She'll mop
up the floor
when she
drops
all the eggs,

and wash off the drawings
she's done on her legs.

Yet no matter
how much
her poor
mother begs,

Ginger McFlea
will **not** clean
her pegs.

Ginger McFlea
will **not**
clean her molars.

She sulks
when she can't
have a big
glass of cola,

and flings herself into
the old baby stroller,

forgetting it tends to be quite a
fast roller!

But Ginger McFlea
will not clean her molars.

Ginger McFlea will **not** clean her incisors.

Says Jasper,

'That plaque on your teeth could win prizes!

Mum's taking you off to our dental advisor. I reckon the state of your **teeth** will surprise her.'

But Ginger McFlea
will **not** clean her incisors.

'Now, Ginger,' says
Doctor Felicity Cheek.
'Lay back in my
chair and I'll
just take
a peek.'

She gasps, 'My dear Ginger,
that mouth is a mess!

Those holes
in your
teeth cause
me dental
distress.'

'Compared to young Jasper whose pegs are pristine,

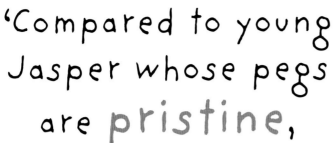

your mouthful of fangs are a dentist's worst dream!'

'Those teeth won't stand up to the tooth fairy test.

She builds fairy houses from only the best,'

'But don't take my word
if you have any doubt,

let's ring up the expert

and sort this mess out?

So Ginger McFlea rings up the tooth fairy.

'Good morning, Tooth Housing,' she says.

'This is Mary.'

And when Ginger asks
if the dentist is right,

she says,
'Yes, I only take teeth
of pure white.'

'I need the best pearlers
for sound fairy dwellings.'

'Bad teeth are
unstable and worse...

end up smelling!'

Ginger McFlea now
cleans all her teeth.

And keeps her toothbrush

from her pet turtle, Keith.

And much to her
mum and dad's

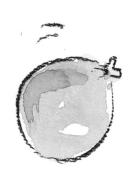

desperate relief,

she doesn't eat lollies,

well...one for a treat.

So now when she's asked for her dental belief,

she says, 'The tooth fairy needs good strong white teeth.'

And thanks to the tooth fairy's fine sense of style,

Ginger McFlea
has a pearly white smile.